by Billy Lopez
illustrated by Amy Marie Stadelmann,
Little Airplane Productions

SIMON SPOTLIGHT/NICKELODEON
New York   London   Toronto   Sydney

Based on the TV series *Nick Jr. Wonder Pets!*™ as seen on Nickelodeon®

SIMON SPOTLIGHT
An imprint of Simon & Schuster Children's Publishing Division
1230 Avenue of the Americas, New York, New York 10020
© 2009 Viacom International Inc. All rights reserved.
NICK JR., *Nick Jr. Wonder Pets!*, and all related titles, logos, and characters are trademarks
of Viacom International Inc.
First Edition
2 4 6 8 10 9 7 5 3 1
Library of Congress Cataloging-in-Publication Data
Lopez, Billy.
Save the egg! / by Billy Lopez ; illustrated by Little Airplane Productions.
p. cm. — (Ready-to-read)
"Based on the TV series Nick Jr. Wonder Pets! as seen on Nick Jr."
ISBN-13: 978-1-4169-7103-0
ISBN-10: 1-4169-7103-3
I. Little Airplane Productions. II. Wonder Pets! (Television program) III. Title.
PZ7.L876348Sav 2009
[E]—dc22
2008010384

Hello!

We are the Wonder Pets.

An egg is on a cliff.

We have to save it!

We are on our way!

Look! The egg!

The egg is falling!

The egg is rolling
into a hole!

Grab the egg!

Look up there!

The egg is up in the air!

Catch the egg!

We saved the egg.

The egg is hatching.

A baby eagle!

A mommy eagle!

Our work here is done!